For Nate, because dinosaurs

—T. M.

For Jurgita

—R. S.

SIMON & SCHUSTER BOOKS FOR YOUNG READERS

An imprint of Simon & Schuster Children's Publishing Division

1230 Avenue of the Americas, New York, New York 10020

Text copyright © 2020 by Tim McCanna

Illustrations copyright © 2020 by Richard Smythe

SIMON & SCHUSTER BOOKS FOR YOUNG READERS is a trademark of Simon & Schuster, Inc.

For information about special discounts for bulk purchases, please contact Simon & Schuster Special Sales at 1-866-506-1949 or business@simonandschuster.com.

The Simon & Schuster Speakers Bureau can bring authors to your live event. For more information or to book an event, contact the Simon & Schuster Speakers Bureau at 1-866-248-3049 or visit our website at www.simonspeakers.com.

Book design by Chloë Foglia

The text for this book is set in Brioso.

The illustrations for this book are rendered in watercolor and finished digitally.

Manufactured in China

0520 SCP

First Edition

10 9 8 7 6 5 4 3 2 1

Names: McCanna, Tim, author. | Smythe, Richard, 1986– illustrator.

Title: Dinosong / written by Tim McCanna ; illustrated by Richard Smythe.

Description: First edition. | New York : Simon & Schuster Books for Young Readers, [2020] | "A Paula Wiseman Book." | Audience: Ages 4–8 | Audience: Grades 2-3 | Summary: Illustrations and easy-to-read, rhyming text follow three dinosaurs—a triceratops, sauropod, and ankylosaur—as they make their way through a dangerous, rock-strewn environment. Includes facts about rocks and minerals.

Identifiers: LCCN 2019028142 (print) | LCCN 2019028143 (eBook) | ISBN 9781534430020 (hardback) | ISBN 9781534430037 (eBook)

Subjects: CYAC: Stories in rhyme. | Dinosaurs—Fiction. | Rocks—Fiction.

Classification: LCC PZ8.3.M13193 Din 2020 (print) | LCC PZ8.3.M13193 (eBook) | DDC [E]—dc23

LC record available at https://lccn.loc.gov/2019028142

A Paula Wiseman Book

Simon & Schuster Books for Young Readers

New York London Toronto Sydney New Delhi

DINOSONG

Tim McCanna

Illustrated by
Richard Smythe

Chip
chop

trip

trop

flunk.

Whack
smack

clank clack

crinkle crackle

clunk.

Moan   creak

groan   squeak

tramp

tromp

bump.

Rumble shiver

grumble quiver

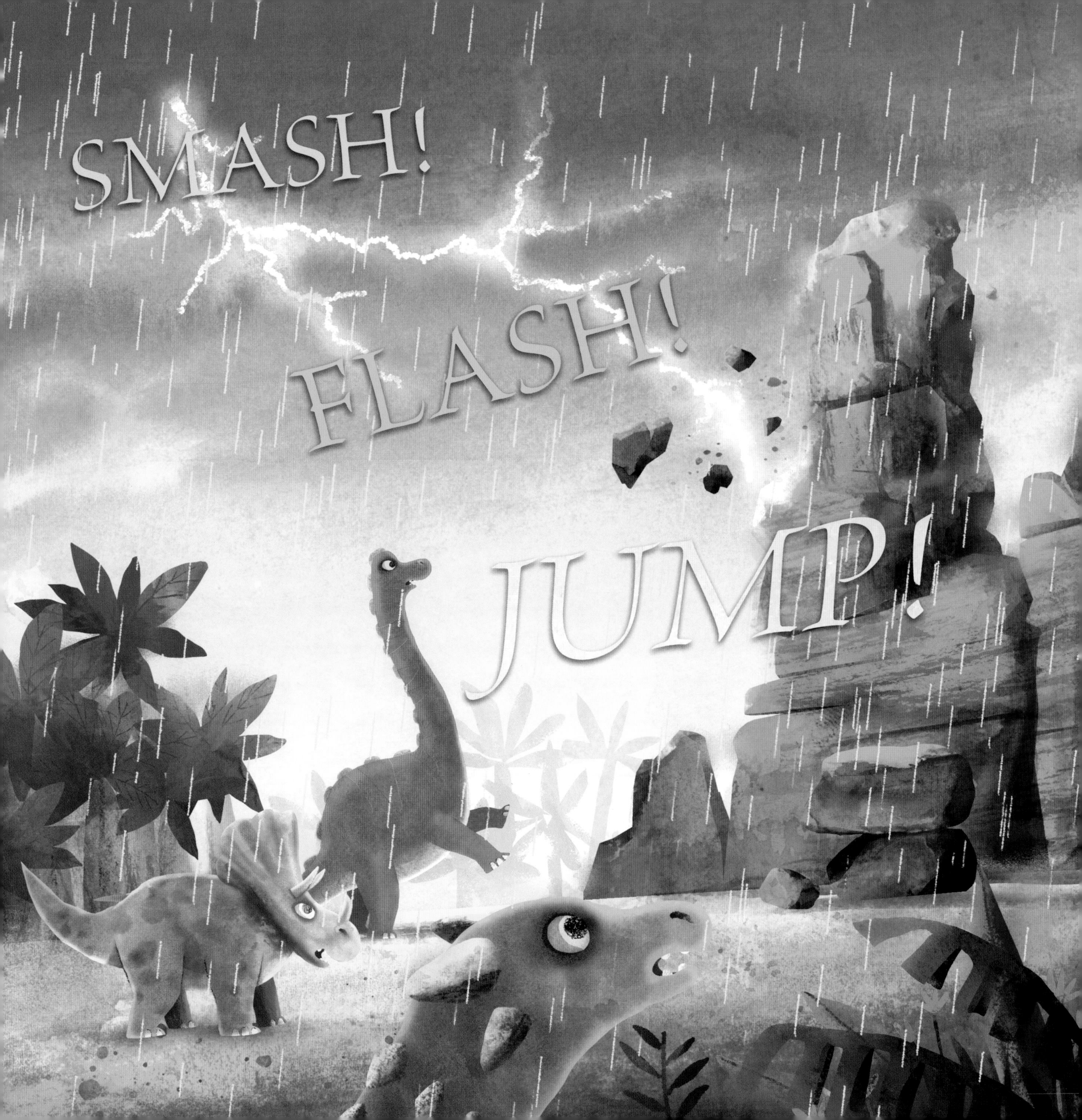
SMASH!
FLASH!
JUMP!

clang roll

quake

shake

zoom.

Sizzle   fizzle

shuffle

scuffle.

BO

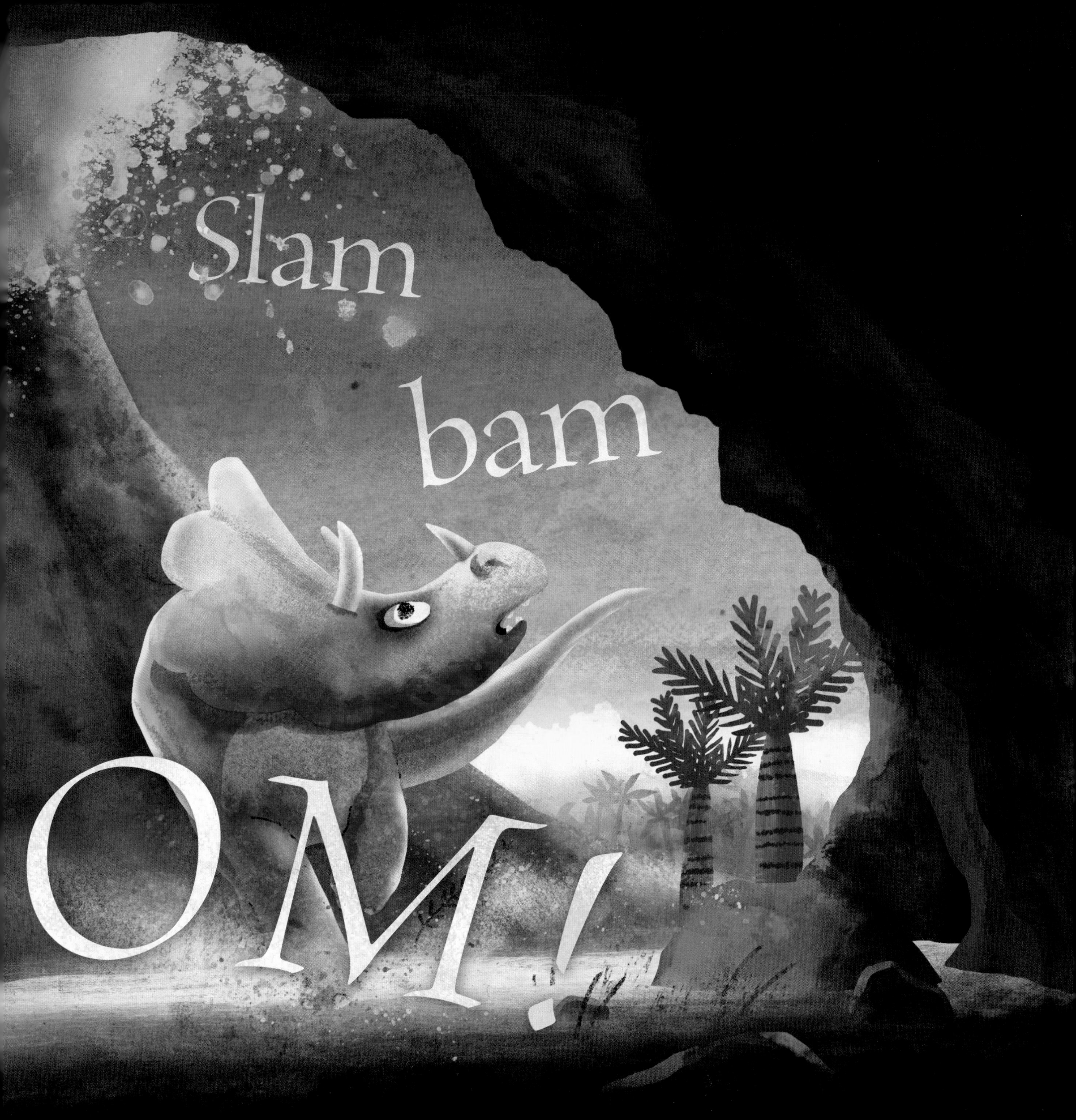
Slam
bam
OM!

Clip

clomp

slip

stomp

bound.

Scribble
scrabble

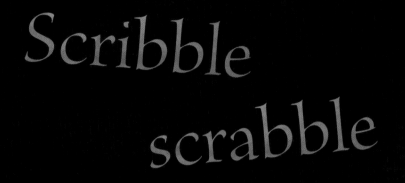

stumble bumble.

Safe and sound.

LISTEN TO THE DINOSONG

Dinosaurs ruled the world for millions of years. These amazing prehistoric creatures may have vanished long ago, but they live on in our imaginations today.

• Can you identify the different dinosaurs in *Dinosong*? Spiky, club-tailed **ankylosaurs**, three-horned **triceratops**, and long-necked **sauropods** all lived roughly 70 million years ago during the late **Cretaceous** period. Flying **pterosaurs** and ostrich-like **ornithomimus** were also prevalent at that time. Many volcanoes exploded around the planet during the Cretaceous period, due to the shifting of Earth's **tectonic plates**.

• Today we have proof of dinosaurs through fossils and footprints. Dinosaur bone fossils were created through a long process called **permineralization**. A dinosaur's bones may have become buried in mud or sand, and over thousands of years, water deposited minerals in place of the original bone material.

• **Paleontologists**, scientists who study fossils of ancient plants and animals, can only guess what a dinosaur's skin actually looked like. Some say it was dull brown or green. Drab skin might have allowed dinosaurs to **camouflage** themselves and hide among plants and rocks. Other research suggests that dinosaurs came in a wide variety of colors with bright markings, or even feathers, in order to recognize each other and attract mates.

• **Magma** is hot, molten rock under the Earth. **Volcanoes** are created when magma shoots out of a mountain onto the surface of the Earth. Molten rock that comes from a volcano is called **lava**. There are around 1,500 potentially active volcanoes on Earth.

• **Stalactites** and **stalagmites** are mineral formations that often occur in caves. Minerals in drips of water from the cave ceiling accumulate very slowly over long stretches of time. Stalactites hang like icicles from the ceiling, while stalagmites rise up from the ground. The shape, size, and color of these formations can vary depending on the type of mineral content, temperature in the cave, and the flow of water.

• There are three main types of rocks on Earth: sedimentary, metamorphic, and igneous. **Sedimentary** rocks are made of tiny rock particles that settle in layers. **Metamorphic** rocks are created by applying extreme heat and pressure to rocks under the Earth. **Igneous** rocks are formed by the cooling and solidifying of molten rock. Through a combination of time, erosion, movement, and other factors, sedimentary, metamorphic, and igneous rocks can transform from one type to another. This process, which happens over thousands of years, is called the **Rock Cycle**.